Pony Express

Risa Brown

Bethany, Missouri

Photo Credits:
Cover © Catherine Oakeson, Library of Congress; Title Page, Pages 7, 8, 11, 17, 19 © National Park Service;
Pages 5, 13, 20, 21, 22 © Library of Congress; Pages 14, 15 © xphomestation.com

Cataloging-in-Publication Data

Brown, Risa W.
    Pony Express / Risa Brown. — 1st ed.
    p. cm. — (National places)

    Includes bibliographical references and index.
    Summary: Describes the Pony Express and the rough
life of riders and horses, from bad weather and wild animals,
to being attacked.
    ISBN-13: 978-1-4242-1371-9 (lib. bdg. : alk. paper)
    ISBN-10: 1-4242-1371-1 (lib. bdg. : alk. paper)
    ISBN-13: 978-1-4242-1461-7 (pbk. : alk. paper)
    ISBN-10: 1-4242-1461-0 (pbk. : alk. paper)

    1. Pony express—History—Juvenile literature.
2. Postal service—United States—History—Juvenile literature.
3. Express service—United States—History—19th century—Juvenile literature.
4. West (U.S.)—History—Juvenile literature. [1. Pony express—History.
2. Postal service—United States—History. 3. West (U.S.)—History.
4. United States—History.] I. Brown, Risa W. II. Title. III. Series.
    HE6375.P65B76 2007
    383'.143'0973—dc22

First edition
© 2007 Fitzgerald Books
802 N. 41st Street, P.O. Box 505
Bethany, MO 64424, U.S.A.
Printed in China
Library of Congress Control Number: 2006940999

Table of Contents

Why Was Mail Slow?

There were no railroads yet, so mail was carried by slow **steamships** or even slower **stagecoaches**. Both took about a month to deliver the mail.

Quick Mail Service

When the Pony Express began in 1860, people were amazed that mail could cross the country in about ten days. That was a really fast time for crossing a wild **frontier**.

Pony Express Route

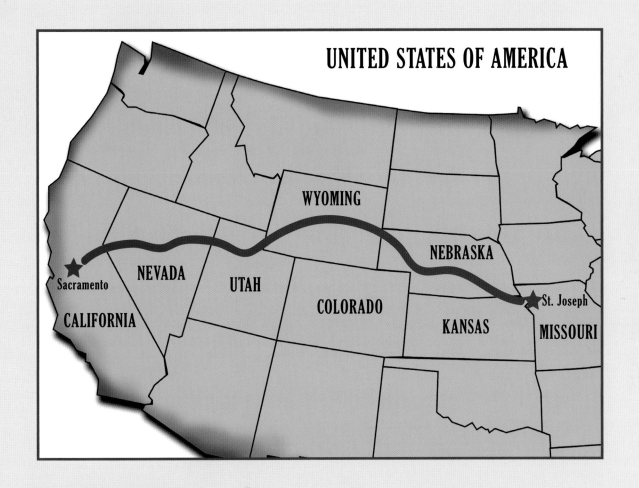

The **route** started in St. Joseph, Missouri and ended in Sacramento, California. This was the shortest route, but it crossed mountains, rivers, and deserts.

Riders

Most riders were men in their teens or twenties. The riders had to be small so they could go as fast as possible.

They had to be brave because they rode day and night. One famous rider was Buffalo Bill Cody.

13

Horses

The horses were tough and mean when not running at top speed. They carried mail in a special bag called a **mochila** that fit over the **saddle**.

Mochila

Relay Stations

Riders stopped at **relay stations** and jumped off a tired horse with the mochila. They threw the mail on a fresh horse and rode off without a break.

17

Dangers

Pony Express riders faced danger from wild animals and harsh weather. Sometimes a horse stumbled and threw the rider.

PONY EXPRESS

THIS MEMORIAL IS THE
PROPERTY OF THE STATE OF COLORADO

DUE NORTH 1235 FEET IS THE ORIGINAL SITE OF

OLD JULESBURG

NAMED FOR JULES BENI WHOSE TRADING
POST WAS ESTABLISHED AT THE "UPPER
CROSSING" OF THE PLATTE PRIOR TO 1860.
JUNCTION OF OREGON AND OVERLAND TRAILS
PONY EXPRESS STATION, 1860-61.
OVERLAND STAGE STATION, 1859-65.
BURNED IN INDIAN RAID, FEB. 2, 1865.

ERECTED BY
THE STATE HISTORICAL SOCIETY OF COLORADO
FROM
THE MRS. J. N. HALL FOUNDATION
AND BY
CITIZENS OF SEDGWICK COUNTY, COLORADO
1931

Native Americans

Native Americans feared the numbers of settlers coming to their land. They attacked Pony Express riders to try to stop the settlers.

End of the Pony Express

The **telegraph** and railroads soon connected the country and news could get to California much quicker, but Pony Express riders excited the whole country.

Glossary

frontier (fruhn TIHOR) — an area without cities

mochila (mo CHILL uh)— a special leather bag designed to carry the mail on a saddle

relay station (REE lay STAY shuhn) — a place where a Pony Express rider exchanged horses

route (ROOT or ROUT) — traveling the same trail or path from one place to another

saddle (SAD uhl) — the seat a rider uses on a horse

stagecoach (STAYJ kohch) — a horse-drawn carriage for carrying people and packages

steamship (STEEM ship) — a ship moved by a steam engine

telegraph (TEL uh graf) — an invention that allowed messages to be sent over wires

Index

FURTHER READING

Dolan, Edward. *The Pony Express.* Benchmark, 2003.
Landau, Elaine. *The Pony Express.* Children's Press, 2006.
Young, Jeff. *The Pony Express and Its Death Defying Mail Carriers.* Enslow, 2006.

WEBSITES TO VISIT

Because Internet links change so often, Fitzgerald Books has developed an online list of websites related to the subject of this book. This site is updated regularly. Please use this link to access the list: www.fitzgeraldbookslinks.com/np/pe

ABOUT THE AUTHOR

Risa Brown was a librarian for twenty years before becoming a full-time writer. Now living in Dallas, she grew up in Midland, Texas, President George W. Bush's hometown.